Cuddle Bear's
BOOK OF
Hugs

Claire Freedman

Gavin Scott

LiTTLE TiGER

LONDON

to:

_____

_____

_____

3SAL

Please return/renew this item by the last date shown
on this label, or on your self-service receipt.

To renew this item, visit **www.librarieswest.org.uk**
or contact your library

Your borrower number and PIN are required.

LibrariesWest

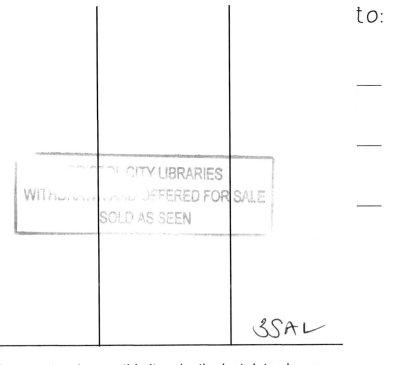

Cuddle Bear LOVES giving hugs,
And bringing cuddly cheer.
But one bear can't hug everyone,
So here's his **great idea**...

HUG ACADEMY

"A school for little bears!" he cheers.
"My **Hug Academy!**
I teach them all my cuddling skills.
Come, peep inside and see!"

"In Cuddle Class," says Cuddle Bear,
"We learn what **hugs** can do.
They **cheer** you up! They make you **smile**,
When you've been feeling **blue!**"

Then Cuddle Bear calls,
"Practice time!

Now, find a
partner, please!

Let's keep it light,
don't hold too **tight**-

A **cuddle**,
not a **squeeze!**"

The bears must all keep **fit** and **strong**,

They work out in the **gym**,

And even **whales** might need a **hug**,
So each bear learns to **swim**.

They practise on an **octopus**,
To get used to the **tickles**.

And **porcupines** need special care,

Because of all their prickles!

Giraffes are **very** hard to reach,
But they **still** need a cuddle.
Frogs are small and **slippery** –
Bears could get in a **muddle**!

Whatever **size**, whatever shape,

From teeny up to **tall**,

Or growly, fluffy, bouncy, shy –

There is a hug for all.

Today at last, it's hug **exams**!
The eager bears make sure
They show off all their cuddling skills
To get a **super** score!

Ready,
teddy,
cuddle!

"**Well done!**" says Cuddle Bear with pride,
"You **ALL** have passed the test.
You've earned a yellow heart that proves
Your cuddles are the **BEST!**"

So if **YOU** want to spread some love,
And show friends that you **care** . . .

...Give someone close a cuddle now,

As hugs are made to SHARE!

To Mark and Ruth, with lots of love
~ C F

For Vics, Laurie and Frida
~ G S

LITTLE TIGER PRESS LTD
an imprint of the Little Tiger Group,
1 Coda Studios, 189 Munster Road, London SW6 6AW
www.littletiger.co.uk
First published in Great Britain 2018
This edition published 2018

Text copyright © Claire Freedman 2018
Illustrations copyright © Gavin Scott 2018

Claire Freedman and Gavin Scott have asserted their rights to be identified
as the author and illustrator of this work under the Copyright,
Designs and Patents Act, 1988.

More cuddly tales from Little Tiger Press!

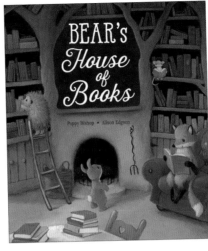

BEAR's House of Books

Poppy Bishop • Alison Edgson

I Love You JUST the Way You Are

TAMMI SALZANO

ADA GREY

Jane Chapman

Love Enough for Two

Tracey Corderoy • Gavin Scott

Little Penguin LOST

Andrea Schomburg & Barbara Röttgen

A Friend Like You

Illustrated by Sean Julian

Stella J Jones   Judi Abbot

With glitter on every page!

GLITTER

For information regarding any of the above titles
or for our catalogue, please contact us:
Little Tiger Press, 1 Coda Studios,
189 Munster Road, London SW6 6AW
Tel: 020 7385 6333
E-mail: contact@littletiger.co.uk
www.littletiger.co.uk